P9-BZK-479

Disney fairies

TinkerBell

Layouts by Art Mawhinney
Art by the Disney Storybook Artists

Published by
Louis Weber, C.E.O., Publications International, Ltd.
7373 North Cicero Avenue, Lincolnwood, Illinois 60712

Ground Floor, 59 Gloucester Place, London W1U 8JJ

Customer Service: 1-800-595-8484 or customer_service@pilbooks.com

www.pilbooks.com

p i kids is a registered trademark of Publications International, Ltd.

Look and Find is a registered trademark of Publications International, Ltd.,
in the United States and in Canada.

8 7 6 5 4 3 2 1

ISBN-13: 978-1-4127-7144-3
ISBN-10: 1-4127-7144-7

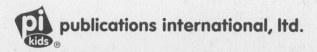

publications international, ltd.

All of the fairies of Pixie Hollow gather to welcome the new arrival. The fairies are curious about Tinker Bell, and she is curious about them, too. Look around the crowd and try to spot these fairies that Tinker Bell will soon meet.

Rosetta

Silvermist

Vidia

Fawn

Iridessa

Bobble

Clank

Tinker Bell discovers that she is a tinker fairy. The tinker fairies help all of the other fairies get ready for spring. Today the tinkers deliver more pots to the pollen fairies. Look around Flower Meadow to find some of the fairies' favorite flowers.

The fairies work hard to fill Springtime Square with all the things they will need to take to the mainland. The Minister of Spring is pleased to announce that everything will be ready in time. But the fairies still have lots of work to do. Look for these ladybugs that the animal fairies are painting.

If you find trouble in Pixie Hollow, you can bet that Vidia isn't far away! When Vidia tricks Tinker Bell into trying to round up the Sprinting Thistles, all of the preparations for spring are ruined. Track down these thistles before they sprint away.

Tink decides to make some new inventions that will help the fairies. She searches the beach for Lost Things that she can use. Hunt for these items that she will bring back to Tinker's Nook.

This metal spring

A button

This gear

This safety pin

A spool

This jingle bell

This screw

A thimble

Tinker Bell saved the day! Her new inventions helped the fairies finish all the preparations for spring. Now that the Everblossom has bloomed, it's time for the fairies to bring spring to the mainland. But they can't do it alone. Look for these buzzing bees that the fairies depend on for help.

Finally, the moment has arrived! The fairies awaken nature with the magic of spring. They get some help from their friends, the birds. Hurry to search for these dazzling snowflakes before they disappear.

Tinker Bell watches the other fairies use their talents to fill the garden with sunshine and flowers. Tink loves all of the colors of spring. Find some of her favorite colors in these butterflies that flutter by.

Each fairy in Pixie Hollow has a special talent, and Tinker Bell will soon discover hers. Return to the Pixie Dust Well to find these objects that represent some of the many different talent groups.

Flower

Leaf

Egg

Droplet of water

Hammer

Lantern

Wooden spoon

Paintbrush

When the fairies bring springtime to the mainland, they will be sure to pack up all their pollen. Fly back to Flower Meadow to find these other things that the fairies will bring for spring.

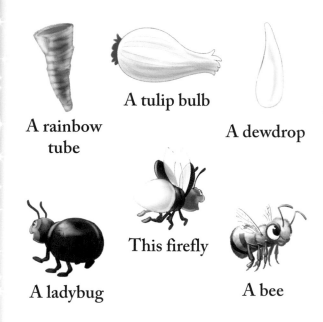

A rainbow tube

A tulip bulb

A dewdrop

A ladybug

This firefly

A bee

Tinker fairies make all the tools that the animal fairies use. Swing back to Springtime Square to find these painting supplies that help give the ladybugs their fresh, new look.

A small pot of black paint

A small pot of red paint

A big pot of black paint

A big pot of red paint

These four paintbrushes

Vidia, the fast-flying fairy, controls the wind and goes everywhere at top speed. Head back to the herd of Sprinting Thistles to find ten whirlwinds that Vidia left in her wake.

Buzz back to the beach to find these items that are not from the mainland. The fairies made them out of things they found in Pixie Hollow.

Woven-grass basket

Blossom lamp

Rose-petal purse

Leaf-and-dewdrop binoculars

Green-leaf shoe

Acorn teapot

Toadstool table

Abacus made from twigs

The fairies have collected lots of supplies to bring with them to the mainland. Fly back to the Everblossom to find these baskets that hold springtime necessities.

Raspberry paint

Blackberry paint

Blueberry paint

Sunflower seeds

Acorns

Pollen

Whenever the fairies travel to the mainland, they make sure to bring some of their favorite things from home. Go back to the snowy gardens to find these things that the fairies brought along for the journey.

A poppy-puff roll

A berry pie

A teacup

A lucky feather

A lantern

A cuddle vine jump rope

A seashell

Even when the fairies are far away, Pixie Hollow is always in their hearts. Spring back to the sunny garden scene and search the clouds for these shapes that remind the fairies of home.

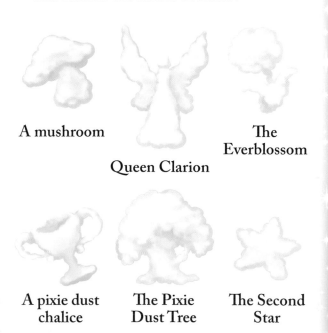

A mushroom

Queen Clarion

The Everblossom

A pixie dust chalice

The Pixie Dust Tree

The Second Star